Chicken Talk Around the World

Carole Lexa Schaefer

Illustrated by Pierr Morgan

little bigfoot
an imprint of sasquatch books
seattle, wa

If your Gram has a farm
near Walla Walla, Washington, United States,
in the morning you find her hens sitting on eggs,
and gather them up—still warm—for breakfast.

The hens—and rooster too—peck at their feed,
fluff, and flap,
and you hear:

Buk-buk.
Bah-bok.

Cock-a-doodle-DOO!
Chicken talk in English.

But if your Gram's farm is tucked into
the outskirts of Mexico City, Mexico,
you call her Abuela (*Ah-BWAY-la*).
Her hens are called las gallinas (*las guy-YEE-nahs*).
Their eggs are los huevos (*los WAY-vohs*).
The rooster is el gallo (*el GUY-yo*).

And as they snap up yellow maize and play in the dust,
you hear:

Co-co-ro-co.
Co-co-ro-co.

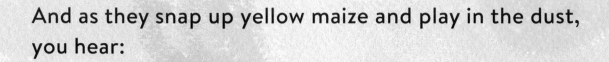

Qui-quiri-QUI!
Chicken talk in Spanish.

Or maybe your Gram's farm nestles
in a small village in Kenya.
You call her Nyanya (*NYAH-nyah*).

And for her hens laying eggs you say:
kuku *(koo-koo)* hutaga *(who-TAH-gah)* mayai *(my-YAI)*.
Kuku *(koo-koo)* is for hens. Hutaga *(who-TAH-gah)* is for laying.
Mayai *(my-YAI)* is for eggs.
And for the rooster, you say—jogoo *(joh-GOH)*.

And as they pick at crusty insects, millet, and kale, you hear:

Koh-koh.
Lee-oh-koh.
KOHHH!

Chicken talk in Swahili.

Or, your Gram's farm might be in the countryside of Honshu, the largest island of Japan.

You call her Obachan (*O-bah-ah-chan*).
Her hens are called mendori (*men-doh-ree*).
Their eggs are tamago (*tah-mah-go*).
The rooster is ondori (*ohn-doh-ree*).

In the yard, they scritch-scratch at the mixed mash,
and you hear:

Ko-ko-ko.
Ko-ko-ko.

Ko-KEH, kok-koh!

Chicken talk in Japanese.

If your Gram's farm covers lush ground
in the state of Bihar, India, you call her Nani (*Naa-nee*).
The hens are her murgi (*mor-ghee*).

The eggs they lay are unda (*un-day*).
The rooster is murga (*mor-gah*).

And as they scuff up the ground
and bob for plump seeds,
you hear:

Ku-ka. Ku-ka.
Ku-ka. Ku-ka.
Ku-ku-doo-koo!

Chicken talk in Hindi.

Your Gram's farm might be among the vineyards of Bordeaux, France. There she's called Grand-mère *(Grahn-mair)*.

Her hens are les poules *(lay POOL-uh)*.
Their eggs are les œufs *(laiz-UHF)*.
The rooster is le coq *(luh KOHK)*.

And as they search around
for grubs and grain—voila! *(vwah-LA)*—
you hear:

Clou, clou.
Clou-ee!

Co-cori-CO!

Chicken talk in French.

In the morning, on that farm near Walla Walla, Washington, you also hear:

"Breakfast time! Eggs are ready!
Hot cakes and syrup too!"

If your Gram, wherever she may be,
calls something like that to you
in her own kind of talk,
run to her and say, "Thanks, Gram."

"Gracias, Abuela!"
("GRAH-see-ahs, Ah-BWAY-la!")

"Asante, Nyanya!"
("Ah-SAHN-tay, NYAH-nyah!")

"Arigato, Obachan!"
("Ah-reh-gah-toh, O-bah-ah-chan!")

"Dhanyawaad, Nani!"
("Dha-nya-vaad, Naa-nee!")

"Merci, Grand-mère!"
("Mair-SEE, Grahn-mair!")

With special thanks to Elly, Jecksen, and Laurence Wanambisi; Said Ramirez; Mari Fujino; Michael Fry; Ameen Dhillon; Anu Garg; Tegan Tigani; and the Kenyan Community Association for their invaluable input

To Janet, Nicola, Susan, Peter, Ranger, and Jon—
good eggs, unique friends, each one
—CLS

For my sister Susan of Walla Walla,
fondly called "Newman" by her grandchildren
—PM

Manufactured in China by C&C Offset Printing Co. Ltd.
Shenzhen, Guangdong Province, in November 2020

LITTLE BIGFOOT with colophon is a registered trademark of Penguin Random House LLC

25 24 23 22 21   9 8 7 6 5 4 3 2 1

Editors: Tegan Tigani, Christy Cox
Production editor: Jill Saginario
Designer: Alicia Terry

Library of Congress Cataloging-in-Publication Data
Names: Schaefer, Carole Lexa, author. | Morgan, Pierr, illustrator.
Title: Chicken talk around the world / Carole Lexa Schaefer ; illustrated by Pierr Morgan.
Description: Seattle, WA : Little Bigfoot, an imprint of Sasquatch Books, [2021] | Audience: Ages 4-8. | Audience: Grades 2-3. | Summary: All around the world, children on their grandmothers' farms listen to the chickens cluck in their own languages.
Identifiers: LCCN 2020019087 | ISBN 9781632172914 (hardcover)
Subjects: CYAC: Chickens--Fiction. | Grandmothers--Fiction. | Animal sounds--Fiction. | Sounds, Words for--Fiction. | Language and languages--Fiction.
Classification: LCC PZ7.S3315 Cf 2021 | DDC [E]--dc23
LC record available at https://lccn.loc.gov/2020019087

ISBN: 978-1-63217-291-4

Sasquatch Books
1904 Third Avenue, Suite 710
Seattle, WA 98101

SasquatchBooks.com